BURTON and DUDLEY

MARJORIE WEINMAN SHARMAT wrote her first poem when she was eight and has been writing ever since. She is the author of many successful books for children. She grew up in Portland, Maine, and is a graduate of Westbrook College. She lives in Irvington, New York, with her husband and two sons.

BARBARA COONEY, whose illustrations have warmed the hearts of children all over the world, won the Caldecott Medal in 1958 for her *Chanticleer and the Fox*. She has illustrated more than eighty books. She lives in Pepperell, Massachusetts.

BURTON
AND
DUDLEY

Marjorie Weinman Sharmat
Illustrated by Barbara Cooney

A CAMELOT BOOK/PUBLISHED BY AVON BOOKS

For my dear cousins,
Dot, Hal, Jon, and Faith Simonds

AVON BOOKS
A division of
The Hearst Corporation
959 Eighth Avenue
New York, New York 10019

Text copyright © 1975 by Marjorie Weinman Sharmat.
Illustrations copyright © 1975 by Barbara Cooney Porter.
Published by arrangement with Holiday House.
Library of Congress Catalog Card Number: 75-1091
ISBN: 0-380-01732-6

First Camelot Printing, August, 1977

CAMELOT TRADEMARK REG. U.S. PAT. OFF. AND IN
OTHER COUNTRIES, MARCA REGISTRADA, HECHO EN
U.S.A.

Printed in the U.S.A.

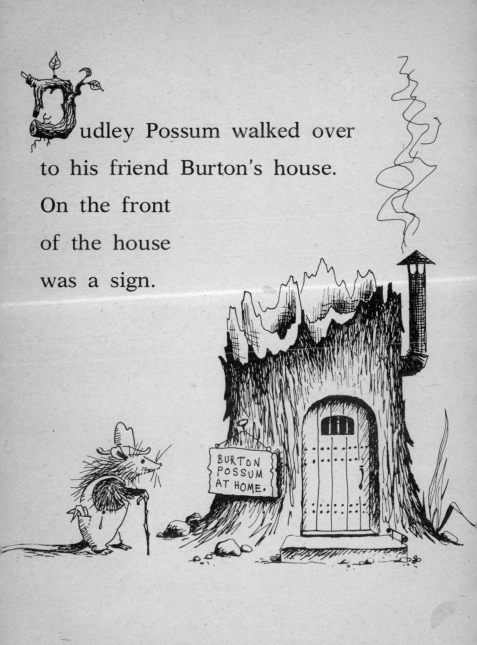

Dudley Possum walked over
to his friend Burton's house.
On the front
of the house
was a sign.

BURTON
POSSUM
AT HOME.

"Yoo hoo, Burton.

Are you home?" called Dudley.

"I am always home," said Burton.
And he opened the door.

Dudley walked in.

"I saw you coming," said Burton,
"so I put on some water for tea."

"I'm not staying," said Dudley.
"I came to ask
if you would like
to take a walk with me."

"A walk?" asked Burton.

"Yes," said Dudley.
"A walk. You know,
when you keep on moving
one foot in front of the other."

"Yes, yes, I know
what a walk is," said Burton.
"And I never take one."

"Well," said Dudley,
"I want you to try.
You hardly ever leave your house.
You need fresh air.
You should feel blood rushing
through your body."

"Why should I feel that?"
asked Burton.
"I feel good not feeling that.
I feel good just looking
out the window.

I feel good watching everyone else getting fresh air."

"Please take a walk
with me," said Dudley.

"I will
if you sit with me for a while
and put your feet up
on a chair," said Burton.
"And look out the window
and feel how wonderful it is
to be inside
with yourself.
And your thoughts.
And your quiet blood."

"It's a deal," said Dudley.

Burton poured some tea
for himself and Dudley.

Then he and Dudley sat
with their feet up on a chair
looking out the window.

"This is the life," said Burton.

"This is leg cramps,"
said Dudley.
"May I put my feet down now?"

"Of course," said Burton.
"The idea is
to relax and drift."

"I relaxed and drifted,"
said Dudley.
"Will you take a walk
with me now?"

"That was the deal," said Burton.

Burton took some magazines,

and Band-aids,

and flea powder,

and a Thermos of tea.

He put them

into his shoulder bag.

He turned his house sign
over to read:

BURTON POSSUM
WILL RETURN
IN AN HOUR.

Then he and Dudley
started to walk.

"There are two kinds of walkers,"
said Dudley.

"Those with a goal

and those who simply walk.

I always have a goal.

Today's goal is a tree.

I heard about a tree

near a brook

twenty miles away.

We will walk to it."

"Anything you say," said Burton.

"Excuse me a moment."

Burton went back
to his house.
He crossed "an hour"
off his sign.
Then he wrote "a day"
and caught up
with Dudley.

BURTON POSSUM
~~WILL~~ RETURN
IN ~~AN HOUR.~~
A DAY

Burton and Dudley
walked along.

"Would you like to hum?"
asked Dudley.

"Not really," said Burton,
"unless you want me to."

"I like to hum
while I walk," said Dudley.
"It sort of
makes me feel zippy."

"Hum for both of us,"
said Burton.

Dudley hummed a song.

"Does that make you feel zippy?"
he asked Burton.

"No," said Burton.
"The deal was
for me to get fresh air
and have blood rushing
through my body.
You didn't say anything
about zippy.
I don't have to feel zippy, do I?"

"Only if you want to,"
said Dudley.

Burton and Dudley walked on.

Then Burton said,
"I feel tired.
Could we please stop
for a few minutes?"

"Of course," said Dudley.
"You're not used to
all of this fresh air."

Burton lay down
on the grass.

"Would it be
asking too much
if you rubbed my stomach?"
Burton asked.
"That always makes me feel good."

"Consider it rubbed,"
said Dudley.

And he bent over
and gently rubbed
Burton's stomach.

"I have known you
for five years.
I have never asked you
to do that before,"
said Burton.

"It's my pleasure,"
said Dudley.

"The sky looks nice
from down here," said Burton.
"I have never seen it
look so nice."

Burton got up.

"I'm feeling better," he said.
"I can go on now."

Burton and Dudley went on.
After a while, Burton stopped.

"I don't suppose
you carry a wet cloth
with you?" he said.
"It isn't something
someone would normally carry."

"I have a scarf.
I can wet it in that stream,"
said Dudley.

"Good," said Burton.

"That would be very helpful
for my splitting headache.
Don't fall into the stream."

Dudley took his scarf
to the stream.
He was careful not to fall in.

"Say, that's a pretty stream,"
said Burton.
"I have never seen
such a pretty stream."

Dudley put the scarf
across Burton's forehead.

"Aaah," said Burton.

"You're a pal.

This is your scarf,

and now it's all soggy."

"It's worth a soggy scarf

to get rid

of your headache,"

said Dudley.

"Thanks," said Burton.

"I can go on now."

Burton and Dudley walked on,

through the forest,

up and down hills,

and across streams.

Suddenly Burton stopped
and sat down.
"I'm tired again," he said.
"Help me."

"I can't," said Dudley.
"I'm tired too."

"*You're* tired?" asked Burton.
"*You,* with all those years
of fresh air
and rushing blood?
You're tired?"

"Yes," said Dudley.
"I am capital T, capital I,
capital R, capital E,
capital D, TIRED!"

"But you're strong," said Burton,
"and sometimes I even think
you're brave.
You can keep going."

"No," said Dudley,
"I am zippy
and I am hopeful
and I am helpful
and that is all I am.
That is my limit.
I have reached my limit."

"Try breathing," said Burton.

"I am breathing," said Dudley.
"I have been breathing
all along."

"I mean *really* breathing,"
said Burton.
"In and out and in and out.
And try to get
your blood excited."

"My blood won't move,"
said Dudley.
"And neither will I."

"Then I'll help you,"
said Burton.
"I've been saving
my energy all these years.
Please stand up."

Dudley stood up.

"Now point yourself
towards where we're going,"
said Burton.

Dudley faced right.

"Now I will push you
while you move
your feet forward.
Are you ready?" asked Burton.

"I'm ready," said Dudley.

Burton pushed Dudley.
Dudley moved his feet ahead.

"It's working!" cried Burton.

"You are doing a good job,"
said Dudley.

Burton pushed Dudley
up and down more hills
and through the woods.

"STOP!" said Dudley suddenly.

"STOP! STOP!

I'm tired.

You push very well,

but I'm more tired than I was
five hills ago."

"I'm not tired," said Burton.
"I like this walk.

I have seen the sky
in a new way.
I have felt the water
from the stream.
I have heard
the singing of the birds.
And I want to see more.
I want to see
the whole world."

"I want to go home," said Dudley.

"Then we will
go home together," said Burton.

"I don't want to see
the whole world
without you."

Through the woods
and up and down hills,
Burton pushed Dudley.

"There's your house,"
said Dudley.

Burton pushed Dudley
into the house.

"Isn't it great

to be home?" asked Dudley.

"No," said Burton.

"Let's take another walk.

Let's walk to the ocean.

And to Spain.

And to London.

And to Iceland.

And to China.

Let's go everywhere."

"Would you mind very much
if we wait until next month
to go everywhere?"
asked Dudley.

"I will wait," said Burton.

"Good," said Dudley.
"In the meantime,
may I borrow your chair
to put my feet on?
And your window
to look out of?"

"Make yourself at home,"
said Burton.

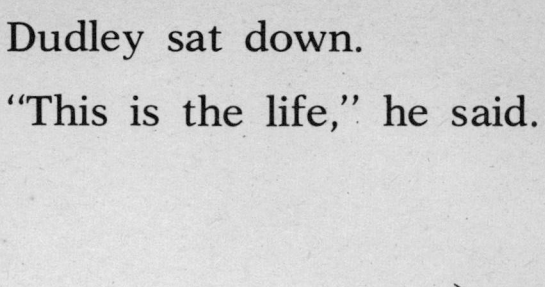

Dudley sat down.

"This is the life," he said.